I'm Brave! I'm Strong! I'm Five!

CARI BEST

ILLUSTRATED BY

BORIS KULIKOV

MARGARET FERGUSON BOOKS
HOLIDAY HOUSE · NEW YORK

Margaret Ferguson Books

Text copyright © 2019 by Cari Best

Illustrations copyright © 2019 by Boris Kulikov

All Rights Reserved

HOLIDAY HOUSE is registered in the U.S. Patent and Trademark Office.

Printed and bound in May 2019 at Tien Wah Press, Johor Bahru, Johor, Malaysia.

The artwork was created with mixed media (watercolor, ink, tea, acryla gouache) on paper.

www.holidayhouse.com

First Edition

1 3 5 7 9 10 8 6 4 2

Library of Congress Cataloging-in-Publication Data

Names: Best, Cari, author. | Kulikov, Boris, 1966– illustrator.

Title: I'm brave! I'm strong! I'm five! / Cari Best ; pictures by Boris Kulikov.

Description: First edition. | New York : Holiday House, [2019] | "Margaret Ferguson Books."

Summary: A five-year-old girl who is brave and strong faces night noises, too much light, and
spooky shadows, all without calling her parents, before finally feeling sleepy.

Identifiers: LCCN 2018036659 | ISBN 9780823443628 (hardcover) | Subjects: | CYAC: Bedtime—Fiction.

Courage—Fiction. Classification: LCC PZ7.B46579 Iaak 2019 | DDC [E]—dc23 LC record available

at https://lccn.loc.gov/2018036659

For Alexandra, who was once brave and strong
and five—and for Ivy who is now   —C. B.

For Max and Andre; and special thanks to Ekaterina Oskolkova,
who helped me with creating the artwork   —B. K.

I've had Mama's stories and Papa's jokes and coffee kisses on both my cheeks.
"It's bedtime now," they said.
But I'm not tired.

I make a star with my flashlight, a car with one headlight,

a lighthouse that blinks on and off.

I wave like a bird and swim like a fish and bounce on my bed like a girl kangaroo that doesn't want to sleep. A phone rings like a marching parade,

a baby cries, and a piano plays. Outside my inside window.
It's so noisy that I go and have a look.

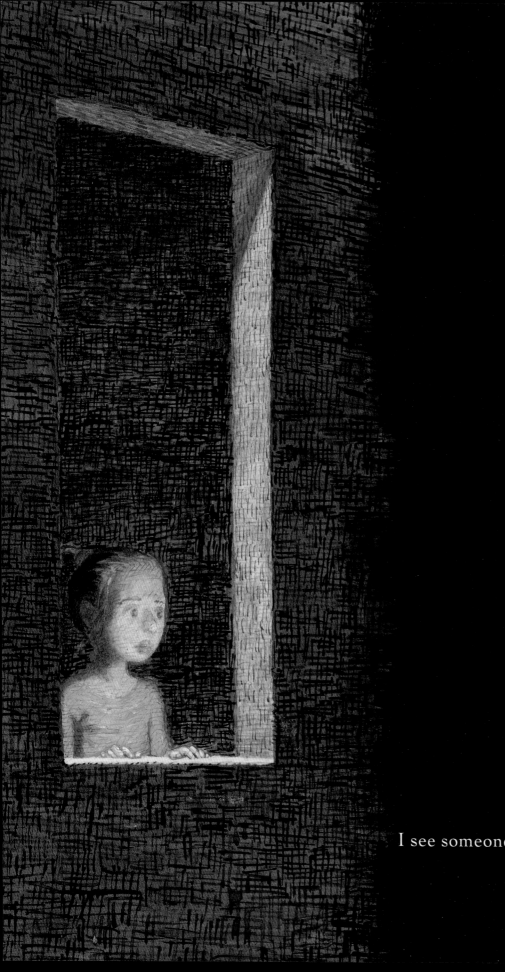

I see someone talking on his phone.

I see Mr. Spock. He's rocking his baby. And Mrs. Bock.
She's playing the piano. Her eyes are closed. But mine aren't

The moon is so white. Like a round ceiling light. A giant eye staring down at me. I could always call Mama. She'd come in with Papa. They'd sing to me till I sleep.

But "No!" I decide. I can do this myself. I'm brave! I'm strong! I'm five!

So I say "Boo!" to the moon.
"I will stop you from staring."

I move my step stool under the window and tug on the curtains—one side is stuck—until both sides come together. That's better!

Now there's a shadow! It's tall with six arms—there on the closet door. I could always call Mama. She'd come in with Papa. They'd shoo the shadow away.

But "No!" I decide. I can do this myself. I'm brave! I'm strong! I'm five!

So I click on my flashlight with a flick of my finger.

Aha! The shadow is my costume — a long leafy tree.
It's for the school play that I'm in about spring.

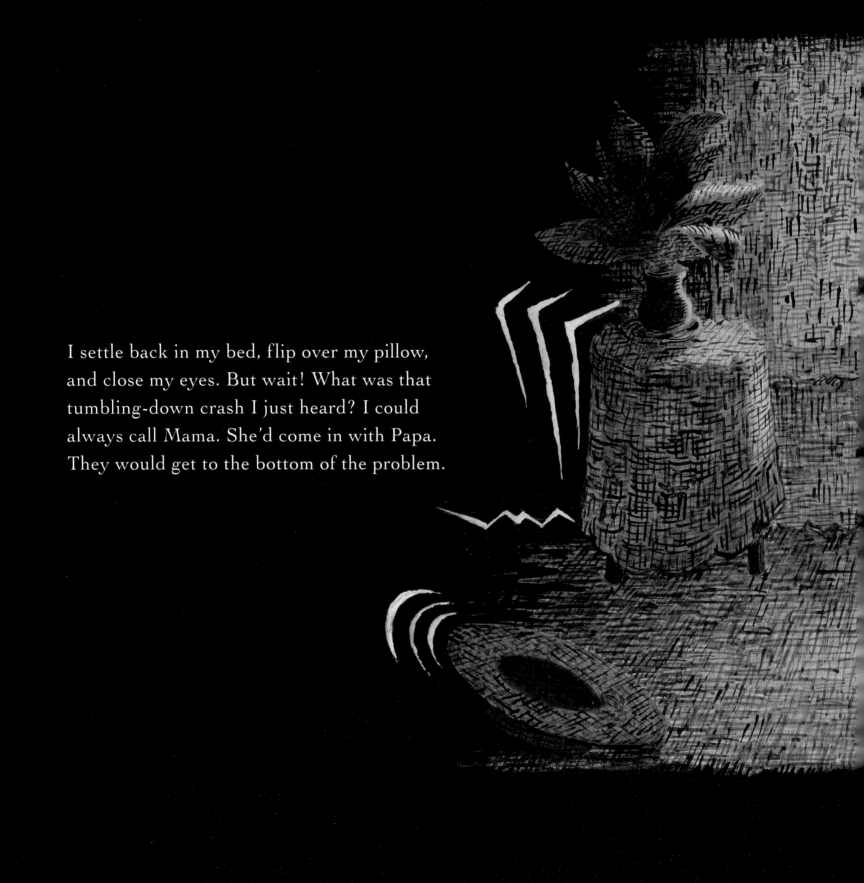

I settle back in my bed, flip over my pillow, and close my eyes. But wait! What was that tumbling-down crash I just heard? I could always call Mama. She'd come in with Papa. They would get to the bottom of the problem.

But "No!" I decide. I can do this myself. I'm brave! I'm strong! I'm five!

So I grab my net and my blanket disguise
as I tiptoe to where the crash came from.

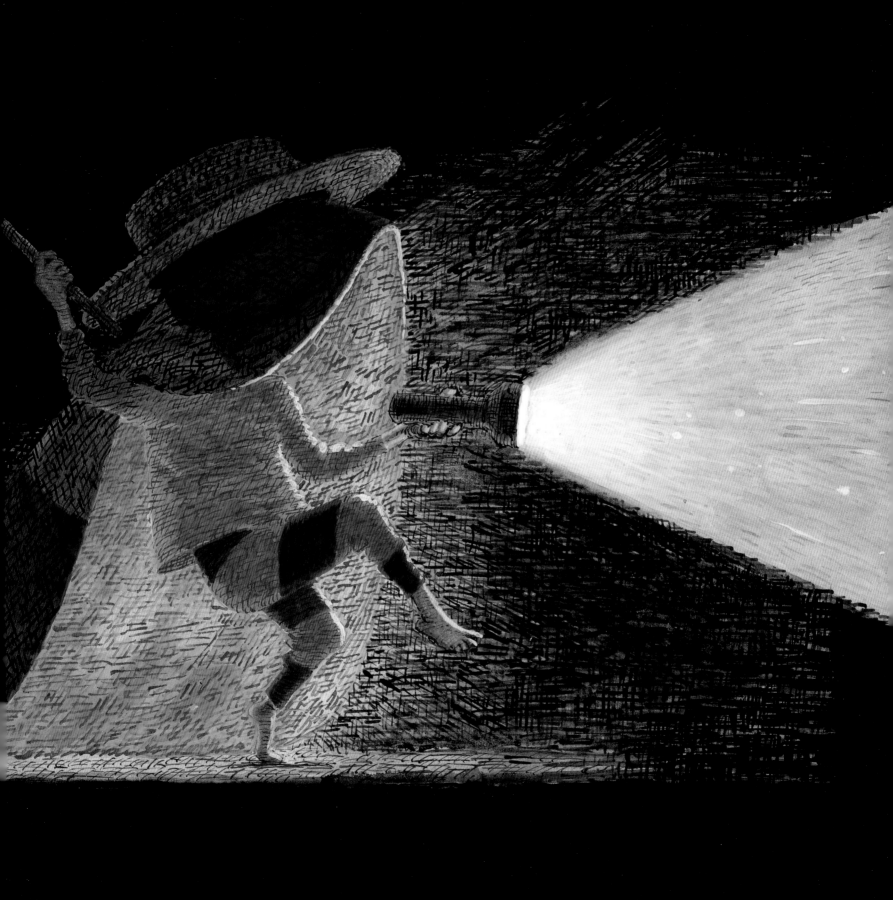

It's only Tuna, my cat! She toppled the mountain of books that I built.

When I find my favorite one on top, I read us both a story.
But I'm still not sleepy!

On my way back to bed, I see a scary face. It has a nose like a ghost,
a mouth like a ghost, and a body I can't see!

I could always call Mama. She'd come in with Papa.
They'd tell me the ghost is friendly.

And they'd be right!

I didn't call Mama. I didn't call Papa. I did everything myself. Hooray!

And now I'm so tired from being brave.

I'm so tired from being strong.

I'm so tired from being five that I'm finally ready to sleep.

Happy good night, everyone!

And happy dreaming, too.